Les Misérables

Les Misérables

By Victor Hugo
Adapted by Monica Kulling

Bullseye Step into Classics™
Random House New York

A BULLSEYE BOOK PUBLISHED BY RANDOM HOUSE, INC.

Text copyright © 1995 by Random House, Inc.

Cover illustration copyright © 1995 by Bill Dodge

Library of Congress Cataloging-in-Publication Data:

Kulling, Monica. Les misérables / by Victor Hugo ; adapted by Monica Kulling.

   p. cm. — (Bullseye step into classics)

SUMMARY: Trying to forget his past and live an honest life, escaped convict Jean Valjean
risks his freedom to take care of a motherless young girl during a period of political
unrest in Paris.

ISBN: 0-679-86668-X [1. France—Fiction. 2. Ex-convicts—Fiction.]

I. Hugo, Victor, 1802-1885. Misérables. II. Title. III. Series. PZ7.K9490155Le 1995
[Fic]—dc20 94-15411

First Random House Bullseye Books edition: 1995

Manufactured in the United States of America   3 4 5 6 7 8 9 10

Contents

Contents

CHAPTER ONE

The Journey's End

Years ago I stole a loaf of bread to feed my hungry family. I was sent to prison and sentenced to hard labor. I traded my name for a number. I was no longer Jean Valjean. For nineteen years, I was known as number 24,601. That was a dark, lonely time for me.

Now I am old and dying. I write this for my daughter, Cosette. When she reads it she will know the truth. I hope she can forgive me. I hope she will understand why I did not tell her everything sooner.

At the time my story begins, I was the breadwinner in my sister's household. Her husband was dead, and she had seven children.

One year the winter was very hard. I didn't have work, and we had no food. I couldn't let the children starve, so I broke the baker's window and stole a loaf of bread. I was twenty-five years old when I lost my freedom.

In October of 1815 I was released from prison. Nineteen years of my life had been spent behind bars.

My first taste of freedom filled me with joy. I was free to walk anywhere!

That first day, I walked many miles. By nightfall my bones ached from the cold, damp air. And I was exhausted.

I stopped at the best inn in the town of Digne. I entered and the innkeeper called, "What can I do for you, monsieur?"

"I want a meal and a bed," I replied. "I have money."

The few francs I had earned in prison were more than enough to pay for food and lodging.

"In that case, you're welcome," said the innkeeper.

I sat down and waited for my dinner. I waited. And waited.

The innkeeper was watching me. He had sent a boy out half an hour ago. At that very moment, the boy was at the police station finding out about me.

"Will dinner be ready soon?" I finally asked. I was faint with hunger.

Just then the boy returned. He handed the innkeeper a scrap of paper. The innkeeper frowned after reading it. He walked over to me.

"I'm sorry, monsieur," he said. "I can't have you here."

"Why?" I asked. "Would you like me to

pay in advance? I have money."

"You may have the money," he replied. "But I don't have the room."

"Then put me in the stable," I begged. I needed sleep desperately.

But even the stable was too good for me. The innkeeper had found out that my name was Jean Valjean. He knew that I carried yellow identity papers, the passport of an ex-convict.

Soon everyone in town knew who I was. No one would rent to me. No one would even give me a glass of water.

I sat outside in the dark and shivered. I had no strength left. But God was watching over me that night. A kind woman stopped and told me to knock at the bishop's house. The good bishop opened his door to me.

The bishop of Digne lived with his sister and a housekeeper. He was a small man of about seventy-five. He lived a quiet, simple life. He had very little, for he gave all his money to the poor.

I told the bishop I was a convict and explained why. I showed him my yellow passport.

"See," I said. "It says I am a dangerous man. I was given five years for robbery and fourteen more for trying to escape four times."

I waited for the bishop to tell me to leave. Instead he invited me to sit at his table. The good silver was laid out. Two silver candlesticks graced the table.

"This isn't my house, but Christ's," he told me. "You are hungry and thirsty, so you are welcome. Everything in my house is yours."

I had never known anyone so generous. What kind of man was this? How could he open his home to me so freely? It scared me. Maybe that's why I did what I did.

I tossed and turned that night. I hadn't slept in a bed for years. At two in the morning, I was wide awake. I had one thought on my mind—the bishop's silver.

It took me an hour to decide. But in the end I did it. I took my shoes off, tiptoed to the cupboard and stole the bishop's silver.

It was a foolish thing to do. The police caught me by dawn. They brought me back to the bishop's house. He spoke before I could say a word.

"I'm delighted to see you again!" he said. "You forgot to take the silver candlesticks with you when you left. I wanted you to have them as well. They're worth a good two hundred francs."

I was stunned. This godly man was forgiving my crime. And he was also giving me his only valuable possessions—his precious silver. It was too much for me. I couldn't believe what was happening.

The police left.

The bishop looked at me and said, "I have bought your soul for God. Promise me you will use the money from this silver to become an honest man."

I was confused when I left the bishop. I wandered the countryside in a daze. I didn't know where I was going. Nor did I care.

Memories of my years in prison flooded my mind. Suddenly I was angry. God had given me such a hard life.

A boy came walking toward me on the footpath. He was flipping a coin. The coin dropped in the dirt just as he passed me. I stamped my foot on it.

"Monsieur, my franc! It's under your foot," the boy pleaded.

I screamed at him to get lost. The look of terror in his eyes was like a wild animal's. I yelled again and the boy bolted.

I did all this without thinking. Then suddenly I saw what I had done. I was a monster! I had stolen from a child!

I broke down and wept. I prayed for forgiveness. I tried to find the boy to make things right. But he was gone.

Oddly, my anger was also gone. The bishop's love had cast it out. I was a changed man. I was truly free for the first time in my life. I have never committed another crime.

CHAPTER TWO

Monsieur Madeleine

I sold most of the silver to set myself up. But I kept the candlesticks to remind me that I was a new man.

I moved to Montreuil-sur-mer. I arrived the night of the town hall fire. The police chief's two children were in the fire. I rescued them. In the excitement, no one asked to see my identity papers.

I changed my name to Madeleine and began a new life.

In three short years I was rich. It happened like this.

The city of Montreuil had a special craft—making black glass beads. The black beads brought Montreuil most of its money. I invented a cheaper glaze to finish the beads. The beads were even more in demand. The town prospered.

I built a bead factory. There was a workshop for men and one for women. Any person wanting honest work could always get a job at my factory.

I gave beds to the hospital and built an old people's home. It was the first one in France. I built a new school.

At first people didn't trust me. They thought I was doing these things for my own gain. How could they know I gave so much because so much had been given to me?

In time I earned everyone's trust. They even made me their mayor. Only one per-

son didn't ...
Javert, the ...
like ice whe...

I lived ...
learn the truth ...
convict. But ...

Soon I ...
like a hawk ... when it came to the law ...
eyes were sharp, and he never let his prey
escape.

One day I was out walking. The ground was soft from rain the day before. I saw a small crowd gathered around a horsecart. They parted when I arrived.

A horse had broken its hind legs and an old man was trapped under the cart. The man was Père Fauchelevent. He had never liked me. I think he was jealous. Once I had been a day laborer, as he was. Now I owned a factory.

"Is help on the way?" I asked.

The loaded cart pressed heavily on the

help didn't arrive soon,
ned.
ned the man next to me.
has gone to get a jack from the
th. But it will take a quarter of an

"A quarter of an hour!" I cried.
"Fauchelevent will be dead in that time.
There's still room for a man to crawl under
the cart and lift it on his back. I'll give five
francs to anyone with the muscle and the
heart."

No one spoke. I raised my offer to ten
francs. Twenty francs. Still no one came
forward. Meanwhile, the cart was sinking
deeper into the mud. It was squeezing the
life out of Fauchelevent.

"A man would have to be as strong as an
ox to lift that load," said Javert.

I had not seen him in the crowd.

"He would risk getting crushed himself,"
he continued. "I have only known one man

who could lift a load like this on his back. I knew him when I was warden in the Toulon prison."

Toulon. How long was it since I'd heard that name spoken? Memories of my years in prison rushed in upon me.

Javert was watching me closely. But I couldn't let Fauchelevent die.

Suddenly the old man cried out, "It's crushing me. My ribs are breaking. For God's sake, do something!"

I stripped off my coat and crawled under the cart. The cart was low in the mud. I was almost flat on my stomach. I slipped again and again, trying to get a foothold.

"Hurry! Come out of there, Monsieur Madeleine!" someone shouted.

Fauchelevent himself cried out, "Go away, Monsieur Madeleine! I'm done for. Let me be, or you'll be killed too."

But I finally had a foothold. I braced the

cart's weight on my back and pushed with all my might.

Slowly, the cart rose. At last the mud-caked wheels came into view! Men from the crowd jumped in to help. The cart was soon out of the mud, and Fauchelevent was rescued.

I got to my feet. Sweat poured down my face. I was drained. As I walked away, I could feel the eyes of the hawk upon my back.

Fauchelevent's kneecap was broken. I bought his horse and cart. I found him work as a gardener in a convent in Paris. In this way, the old man became my friend.

CHAPTER THREE

Fantine

One day Javert arrested a young woman for disturbing the peace. He gave her six months in prison. She had been living on the streets in terrible poverty. Her name was Fantine.

A rich young man had accused her of attacking him. But I had seen what happened from across the street. The man had put a handful of snow down the woman's back. And she had lashed out in anger.

I entered Javert's office. Fantine turned and glared at me.

"So you're the mayor, are you?" she said. Then she spat in my face in fury.

She hated Monsieur Madeleine. She believed she had lost her job because of me. But I didn't know her story.

The woman in charge of the workers in my factory learned that Fantine had a child but wasn't married. She fired her.

"Inspector Javert, this woman is to go free," I said.

Javert was stunned.

"This woman has insulted a respectable citizen," he said.

"I saw the whole thing from across the street," I replied. "The respectable citizen is at fault."

"She has insulted you too. You are the mayor of this town!" said Javert.

"That is my affair," I said. "This woman

will not serve a single day in prison."

"But that's not right," said Javert.

"Enough!" I ordered. "Kindly leave your post."

For a moment Javert didn't know what to do. Then he bowed low and left the room.

Fantine had followed the argument with interest and surprise. She wasn't angry anymore.

"I will see to it that you have what money you need," I told her. "Your worries are over."

This news was too much for the poor woman. She fainted at my feet. Her head burned with fever.

I took Fantine to the factory's nursing station. Her fever raged all night. But by morning it had broken.

"I'm feeling better," said Fantine when I asked how she was.

"I've slept well. I'm sure it was nothing serious. I only wish my daughter Cosette were here with me."

Cosette lived with a family called Thénardier. They owned a tavern in Montfermeil, a town outside Paris. Fantine sent money each month for her daughter's care.

"I left Paris poor," Fantine told me. "I wasn't married to Cosette's father so I had no help from him. I wanted to return to my hometown, Montreuil. There was a new factory. But what could I do with Cosette? The Thénardiers offered to take her until I was settled.

"They wanted seven francs a month for her upkeep. At first, I was able to pay it. I had work in the factory. I even had money to buy new furniture.

"But then Monsieur Thénardier demanded more. He wanted twelve francs, then fifteen. He always had a good reason. Cosette needed a woolen dress for winter.

Cosette was sick. Doctor's bills and medicine put me behind in my payments.

"Things got worse when I lost my job," she continued. "I had to get money any way I could. I sold my beautiful hair. I even sold my two front teeth, as you see.

"I owe Monsieur Thénardier so much money. I'm afraid Cosette may at this moment be living in the street!"

As Fantine finished her story, pain filled her eyes. Her face was thin and as white as the sheets she lay on.

"I will take care of everything," I told her. "You don't have to worry."

Fantine owed Thénardier a hundred and twenty francs. I sent three hundred and told him to use the rest to bring Cosette to me. But Thénardier wrote back asking for more money.

This man was not the kind soul Fantine believed him to be. He was a crook. He thought he had found the goose that laid the golden egg. I had to get Cosette away from him as soon as possible.

Fantine's winter cough turned into pneumonia. One morning the nurse took me aside. "You'd better bring the child," she whispered. "Her mother grows weaker every day."

Fantine opened her eyes and asked for Cosette.

"I will get her myself if I have to," I promised.

I wrote the Thénardiers. Fantine told me what to write. And then she signed it. The letter read:

Monsieur Thénardier,

Please hand Cosette over to the person who brings you this letter. Everything I owe will be paid.

I send you my regards.

Fantine

But my trip was not to be. The next day my dead and buried past would rise to haunt me. And my plan to get Cosette would be delayed.

CHAPTER FOUR

"I Am Jean Valjean"

I was in my office finishing a few things before leaving to get Cosette. Javert was announced.

"Show him in," I said.

When Javert entered, I did not look up. I could not forget how badly he had treated Fantine.

Javert stood there for quite some time. I

don't know how he looked. My eyes were on my paper. Finally, I put my pen down.

"Well, Javert, what is it?" I asked.

"Monsieur Mayor," began Javert. "I wish to speak with you of a serious matter. A rule has been broken."

"What rule?" I asked.

"Someone in the lower ranks has shown disrespect for someone in the higher ranks," he replied.

"Who is the person?" I asked.

"Myself," said Javert.

"You?"

I did not know what Javert was getting at. But I didn't trust him.

"And who has been treated with disrespect?"

"You have, Monsieur Mayor," replied Javert.

Now I was completely baffled. I stood up. Javert's eyes were lowered.

"I have come to ask you to dismiss me," he continued.

My mouth was open. But I couldn't find words. Javert continued.

"You may say I can quit. But that would not be enough. I must be punished. I must be dismissed," said Javert. "I must leave in disgrace."

"What in the world are you talking about?" I asked. "What have you done?"

"I will explain, Monsieur Mayor," he said. "I was so angry with you six weeks ago, over that woman, that I reported you to the chief of police in Paris."

Now I laughed. It was a mistake after all.

"You reported me?" I replied. "As what? As a mayor who stepped on your toes and took a prisoner from you?"

"No," he said. "As an ex-convict."

The words hit me like a punch in the

stomach. But Javert was still talking, staring at the floor.

"It came to me some time ago," he said. "You look like a prisoner I knew twenty years ago. You walk with a slight limp, as he did. You have his great physical strength. I saw that when you lifted the cart.

"I suspected you of being a man called Jean Valjean."

I dropped back into my chair. I returned to my work.

"And what did the Paris police have to say?" I asked, pretending not to be very interested.

"They said I was crazy," replied Javert. "They told me the real Jean Valjean has been found."

The sheet of paper fell from my hand. I looked hard into Javert's eyes. "Really?" I said without blinking.

"A man called Champmathieu has been

arrested for stealing apples," explained Javert. "When the prisoner was moved to Arras an old inmate recognized him. He said he knew the man to be an ex-convict. He said he knew him in the Toulon prison. In Toulon they found two more convicts who said that this Champmathieu is, in fact, Jean Valjean.

"He is the same age, the same build, and looks like him. I recognized him myself when I went to see him."

"And what does this man say?" I wanted to know.

"Valjean is in a hopeless position," said Javert. "Oddly he doesn't rant and rave as you would expect. He acts as if he doesn't know what's going on. He says over and over: 'My name's Champmathieu, and that is all I have to say.'

"If he is indeed Jean Valjean, it won't go well for him at the trial," continued Javert.

"Stealing apples is a boy's prank. But this man is an ex-convict. Then there's the matter of a boy he robbed."

The trial was to be in Arras—a day's journey away. Javert would be going as a witness.

"Sentence will be passed tomorrow evening at the latest," he said. "Monsieur Mayor, I remind you that I must be dismissed. It was wrong for me to act as I did."

I rose to my feet.

"You deserve to go up in the world, not down," I said. "The offense is not so great. Stay in your present post."

"Monsieur Mayor, I cannot agree to that," he replied. "In my life, I have punished people when they did wrong. It was the just thing to do. Now *I* have done something wrong. You *should* punish me!

"Do not be kind to me, Monsieur Mayor," Javert said quietly. "I do not believe in kindness. I believe in justice."

"This is a matter for me to decide," I said. "And I have decided. Stay where you are."

Bowing low, Javert turned to leave. At the door he paused, "I will stay, Monsieur Mayor, until I have been replaced."

Javert left, and I was alone with my thoughts. It was a difficult choice. I knew what waited for me in prison. Long days and years of hardship. The ball and the chain dragging at my leg. A wooden board for a bed. The whip if one so much as lifted an eyebrow.

I knew what I would be going back to. But I also knew I couldn't let an innocent man go to prison in my place. I rented a horse and buggy and left for Arras in the early morning.

I raced the horse the whole way and arrived in Arras just as Champmathieu took the stand. Because I was a mayor, I was seated at the front of the courtroom. I searched the room for Javert. But I couldn't find him.

The accused stood in front of the judge. He twisted a grimy cap in his hands. He was frightened and confused.

I recognized the three witnesses. They were men I knew years ago in Toulon. Their names were Brevet, Chenildieu, and Cochepaille.

Each one told the court that the man before them was Jean Valjean. Only Champmathieu and I knew he was innocent.

This man would soon be sent to prison for the rest of his life for crimes he didn't commit. I had to speak.

"Brevet, Chenildieu, and Cochepaille, look at me!" I shouted. "Don't you recognize me? Don't you know who I am?"

The courtroom was silent.

"*I* am Jean Valjean," I told the court. "I am the man.

"Brevet, remember the suspenders you used to wear?" I asked. "They had stripes. Do you remember?"

Brevet gave a start of surprise. He stared at me wide-eyed.

"And you, Chenildieu," I continued. "You have a bad scar on your right shoulder. You burnt it on a hot stove."

"It's the truth," said Chenildieu.

I turned to Cochepaille. "On your left elbow, Cochepaille, there's a tattoo in blue lettering. It reads '1 March 1815'—the date of Napoleon's landing at Cannes. Pull up your sleeve. Show us."

Cochepaille did as I asked. There was the tattoo, just as I had said.

"Now do you believe that I am Jean

Valjean? Champmathieu is innocent.

"I have things to do," I said. "The Court knows who I am and where I live. You can come for me when you choose."

I left Arras to return to Fantine.

CHAPTER FIVE

Number 9,430

"Monsieur Mayor, what has happened to you?" said the nurse. A look of shock was on her face. "Your hair is completely white."

I looked in a mirror. It was true. My hair was white. The courtroom had been hard on me. But I had a more pressing concern: Fantine.

"How is Fantine? May I see her?"

I was led to Fantine's bedside. She was

sinking fast. Her eyes opened and she greeted me warmly.

"I knew you were here," she said. "I could see you in my sleep. And where is my Cosette? Why isn't she sitting on the bed waiting for me?"

"You must keep calm, my child," I said. "Your little girl is here."

I was lying. But I wanted her to keep calm.

"Oh, please," she cried. Her eyes were bright and her hands were clasped. "Won't someone bring her in?"

"Not yet," I said.

"You have to rest first," said the doctor. He had come in to check on her. "You still have a fever. Such excitement wouldn't be good for you."

"First you must get well," I agreed. "Then you can see your girl."

I hoped my words would comfort her. I

wanted her to sleep. Then I could go and get Cosette.

But my words made her more upset.

"I want to see my baby! How can you be so foolish? Let me see my Cosette!" she begged.

"You see how quickly you get upset," said the doctor. "As long as you are like this, I can't let you see your child. It's not enough to see her. You have to live for her."

I held Fantine's hand. She seemed to be in another world. Her eyes were looking upward.

"I can hear her!" she cried. "It's my darling Cosette. I can hear her."

She pointed over my shoulder. "It's him. It's him. He's come to get me!"

I turned to see who she pointed at. It was Javert. He had entered the room silently and was waiting for me.

Fantine sat up in bed. "Monsieur

Madeleine, save me!" Then she fell back against the pillow. Her head hit the headboard. It sank limply against her shoulder. Her mouth was open. Her eyes were sightless. She was dead.

"You have killed this woman," I said to Javert.

"Let's go!" he ordered. "We've wasted enough time. March! Or I'll put the handcuffs on you."

I set Fantine's head gently on the pillow. I tucked her hair in her cap and closed her eyes. I kissed the hand that hung over the bed and laid it on top of the other one.

I rose to my feet.

"I am at your service," I said.

Javert put me in the town lockup. He intended to take me to Toulon in the morning. But I had other plans. I broke a window bar and dropped down from the roof.

I ran home and found my metal savings

box. It had all my money in it. I wrapped the silver candlesticks in an old shirt. I buried both in the woods nearby.

Then I fled to Paris, hoping to disappear in the great city. But the Paris police searched for me. They asked Javert to help them locate me. He was relentless. I was caught.

My new number was 9,430. Would I wear it as long as my first number? Was I doomed to labor in shackles in the prison at Toulon until my death? I had no answers to these questions.

But there came a day when my life took another turn. This is how it happened.

The warship *Orion* came to Toulon harbor to be repaired. I was one of a crew of prisoners who was sent to help clean her hull. She was a big ship, and the crowds came out to watch.

Suddenly one of the seamen of the *Orion*

fell from a topsail. During his fall, his hands got tangled on one of the sail's ropes. He was hundreds of feet above the sea. He hung like a stone in a sling.

No one came to his rescue. He was wriggling and weakening. I knew he would soon drop into the sea. I made up my mind. I would try to rescue the seaman.

I asked the officer on duty if he would break my ankle chain. I grabbed a rope and dashed up the rigging. As everybody watched, I raced across the outer part of the sail.

I tied the rope to the sail and lowered myself to the seaman's level.

Now two of us hung above the sea.

The seaman was getting tired. He would soon let go. Quickly, I tied the rope around his middle and climbed back up. I pulled the seaman up. He was carried to safety.

But I was weak from the rescue. I

staggered on the outer part of the sail. Then I fell into the sea. I would not go back to the ship or to prison. I would take my chances in the water.

As I fell, I heard the cry of the crowd. The next day the paper reported my death:

17 November 1823. Yesterday a convict working on the *Orion* fell into the sea. He was drowned after rescuing a crew member. The body was not recovered. The man's number was 9,430. His name was Jean Valjean.

CHAPTER SIX

Cosette

But drowning was not my fate. I had made a promise, and I meant to keep it.

I dug up my money and the candlesticks. I dressed as a poor man. No one would have known that the man walking the road to Montfermeil was once Monsieur Madeleine, the mayor.

The Thénardiers' inn was called The Sergeant of Waterloo. The sign over the door showed a soldier carrying another soldier on his back.

I was nearing the inn when I saw a little girl. She was you, my dear Cosette. You were carrying a big bucket of water. You were only eight. But the Thénardiers worked you like a horse.

The bucket of water was heavy. The small girl put it down every few steps and rested.

"Oh, God help me! Please, dear God!" she sobbed.

I came up from behind and reached down for the handle. I didn't say a word. The girl looked up, unafraid. She trusted me.

"Have you carried this far?" I asked her.

"From the spring back there," she replied.

"Haven't you a mother?" I asked.

"I don't think I've ever had one," the

child replied. "The others have a mother. But I have not."

"What others?" I asked.

"Madame Thénardier's children," she said. "She has two girls. Their names are Éponine and Azelma."

"And what do they do?" I asked.

"Oh, they have lovely dolls," she replied. "They play games all day."

"And what do you do?"

"I work," she said, her eyes filled with tears. "I haven't got many toys. And Ponine and Zelma won't let me play with their dolls."

We were almost at the inn door. Cosette asked me for the bucket.

"If Madame sees someone carrying it for me, she'll beat me."

I gave her the bucket, and we entered the noisy inn.

Madame Thénardier came to the door

carrying a candle. She was a big woman. Her features were coarse. She looked as though she rarely smiled.

"So there you are, you good-for-nothing," she said to Cosette. "You've taken your time again. I guess you were fooling around as usual."

"Madame," said Cosette, trembling. "Here is a gentleman who wants a room for the night."

Madame Thénardier thought I was a beggar without any money.

"The rooms are full," she said.

"You can put me where you like," I offered. "In the hayloft or the stable. I'll pay the same price as for a room."

"Very well, forty francs," she said.

The price was too high. But I agreed. I put my bundle and my walking stick on a bench and sat down. Cosette brought me wine and a glass. Then she crawled under a table on the other side of the room.

Cosette knit and chewed her lower lip. She watched the sisters play with their dolls near the fireplace.

She was a plain child. She would have been pretty if she were happy. Too much work and too little food had made her thin and pale. Her large blue eyes had deep shadows under them.

Her dress was a rag, hardly warm enough for summer, let alone winter. She looked like a shivering, frightened rabbit.

"Cosette!" called Madame Thénardier.

Cosette had forgotten to buy bread. Madame wanted her money back. Cosette stuffed her hand into her apron pocket. Her face fell. The coin was gone. She had lost it.

"So you've lost it, have you?" said Madame Thénardier. "Or are you trying to steal it?"

Madame Thénardier reached for the strap hanging on the chimney. She raised it above Cosette's head.

"Please, Madame! Please!" cried the frightened girl.

I took a coin from my vest pocket. No one saw me put it on the floor.

"Pardon me, Madame," I said. "The coin rolled under my table. It must have fallen from the child's pocket."

Madame Thénardier snatched the money from my hand. She put it in her pocket and glared at Cosette. Cosette ran back under the table. She sent me a look of thanks.

I had seen a doll in a store window on my way into town. It was bigger and much more beautiful than the one the sisters were playing with. I left the inn and went to the store. I bought the doll for Cosette.

"Here, it's for you," I said, holding it out to her.

Cosette was dazzled. The doll had a beautiful pink dress. Cosette's face was like a burst of sunshine.

Madame Thénardier, Éponine, and Azelma stared like statues. The room was silent. Madame Thénardier might have been thinking: Who *is* this man? Is he a beggar or a millionaire? Or worse, is he a criminal?

"Is it true, monsieur?" asked Cosette. "Is the lady really mine?"

This poor child brought me close to tears. I could only nod and put the doll into her hands.

"I'll call her Catherine," she said.

Cosette played with the doll until her bedtime. She went to sleep in her torn dress to keep warm.

I was up early the next morning. Madame Thénardier handed me my bill. It was high. But I paid it without a word. I had other things on my mind.

"We have so many expenses, monsieur," said Madame Thénardier. She had seen the look I gave the bill. "There's the child. You saw her last night. She costs a pretty penny to keep. And I have my own daughters to consider."

"Suppose I took her off your hands?" I said.

"What—Cosette?"

"Yes."

"Why, monsieur, my dear monsieur, take her!" Madame Thénardier's face was red with excitement. "Take her away. Take care of her, spoil her, and may you be blessed!"

But Monsieur Thénardier wasn't so pleased. He was listening from the hall. He didn't want to let the child go.

"I can't allow it," he said, entering the room.

"It is true that she costs money and that we are not rich. I had to pay over four hundred francs for one of her illnesses. But I love the child and so does my wife. We need to see her running about the place."

Monsieur Thénardier took fifteen hundred francs for Cosette.

I gave the child a bundle of warm clothes that I had brought for her. She came downstairs dressed all in black. She carried her doll in one hand and took my hand with the other. We left the inn.

We hadn't gone far down the road when the innkeeper caught up with us.

"I can't let you take the child without permission from her mother," said Thénardier. "Give her back to me."

He wanted more money. But I had a surprise for him. I had Fantine's letter. Thénardier recognized her writing.

But still he demanded more money. I reached for Cosette with one hand and gripped my heavy walking stick with the other. Thénardier didn't stay to see what I could do with it.

Cosette and I turned and walked toward our future.

CHAPTER SEVEN

Night Hunt

Cosette and I moved into an apartment in the poorest part of Paris. Few people lived in our run-down building. It was perfect for us. No one would ever find us here.

We lived a quiet life. For the first time in her young life, Cosette could play and forget about work.

How I came to love my Cosette! I had never loved anything or anyone before. I had never been a father, a lover, a husband, or even a friend.

Cosette's love gave me hope. She became my daughter. And I became her father. Sometimes I thought my heart would burst with tenderness.

Weeks passed. I was content. In the mornings I taught Cosette how to read. In the afternoons she played with her doll. I loved to watch her.

We couldn't risk going out during the day. So we took our walks in the evenings.

I still dressed like a poor man. And that's what people thought I was. They didn't know I had my money sewn into the lining of my coat. I could get to it whenever I needed it.

Each evening I gave a coin to a beggar sitting by a church. One evening something happened that changed our lives.

The beggar sat on the sidewalk as usual. I dropped a coin into his open palm. He looked up for a moment. Then quickly bowed his head.

In that moment, I thought I saw the face of a man I never wanted to see again—Javert! But surely the streetlamp was playing tricks with my eyes.

At home, I couldn't get the beggar out of my mind. I needed to speak to him. That way I would know for sure if it was Javert.

The next evening when I gave my coin, I spoke.

"Good evening, old man," I said, dropping a coin into his palm.

"Thank you, thank you, kind sir," he replied.

The old beggar's face stared up at me. It wasn't Javert after all. My eyes *had* been playing tricks on me.

A few nights later I heard the front door open. It was usually locked at that time. I sent Cosette to her room and told her to be quiet.

A man was climbing the stairs. I blew out my candle and sat on a chair, silent. The man stopped outside my door. I held my breath.

He had a candle. A gleam of light shone under my door. The man walked down the hall and closed a door. I threw myself on my bed and didn't shut my eyes all night.

At daybreak, the same door opened. I kneeled to peer through my keyhole. I couldn't see the man's face. His outline told me all I needed to know. It was Javert!

At dusk that same day, Cosette and I left our apartment. The moon was full.

We ran down a street. Then turned to run back up it. In this way, I hoped Javert would lose our trail.

Cosette stayed close. She didn't ask questions. I didn't know where I was going. I was trusting God as Cosette was trusting me.

Were we being followed? I didn't know. Did Javert know that I was Jean Valjean? I didn't know that either. I only knew I didn't want to stay around to find out.

We passed a church. Its bell chimed eleven o'clock. We passed a police station. Three men stood outside. As we passed, one went inside.

We ducked down a side street and hid in a doorway. The man who had gone inside came out with a fourth man. The moon lit their faces. The new man was Javert!

We left the doorway and ran to a small bridge. By now Cosette was tired. I carried her across and then looked back. The four men were hurrying across the bridge!

We ran down a lane between stone walls. After only a few yards, the lane forked. I chose the right fork because it led away from the city.

I could hear Javert and his men running behind us.

Suddenly the lane ended with a stone wall! We couldn't go forward and we couldn't go back. And Javert's men were closing in on us! There was only one way to go—up.

I had been a strong climber in prison. I escaped three times by climbing stone walls with only my bare hands and feet. But Cosette couldn't climb the wall by herself. And I wouldn't make it up the wall with her on my back.

"I'm frightened, Father," she said. "Who's that coming?"

I put Cosette down.

"It's Madame Thénardier," I lied. I wanted Cosette to do as I told her.

"Don't talk," I said. "Leave everything to me. If you make a sound, she'll hear you. She wants you back."

To climb the wall with Cosette, I needed a rope. But where could I get one quickly? Then I remembered. The streetlamp! Each streetlamp in Paris was raised and lowered by a rope. Without another word, I raced to the streetlamp at the end of the alley, took the coil of rope, and hurried back to Cosette.

There was no time to lose. I took off my scarf and looped one end under Cosette's arms. I tied the other end to my rope. Then I took off my shoes and socks and threw them over the wall. I was on top of the wall in half a minute.

Cosette stared up at me, amazed. She was frozen into silence by the thought of Madame Thénardier.

I pulled Cosette to the top and put her on my back. I held both her hands in one of mine. Then I crawled on my stomach along the top of the wall.

We came to the roof of a small building. I slid onto the roof without letting go of the wall. Javert was running down the lane, shouting, "Search the dead end! He won't escape me this time!"

The police raced to the end of the lane. I let go and coasted down the roof with Cosette still on my back. A tree stopped us from dropping to the ground.

We climbed down. We were in the garden of a convent. An old gardener was bent over his roses.

"Here's a hundred francs," I said. "Please let us stay the night."

The moonlight shone on my face.

"Why, it's you, Monsieur Madeleine!" exclaimed the gardener. "Don't you remember me?"

It was Fauchelevent! The man I had rescued from under the horsecart years before.

Chapter Eight

Meeting Marius

I had saved Fauchelevent once. Now he saved me. He said I was his brother. The nuns gave me a job as his helper.

Javert spent months looking for me. But he never searched the convent. In time, he gave up looking.

Cosette joined the convent school and lived with the other girls. I visited her each day. We spent many peaceful years together this way.

I would have been happy if Cosette had wanted to become a nun. I was safe in the convent and could live out my life in peace behind its walls.

But Cosette needed to see the outside world. When she finished school, we moved back into the city.

I bought a house near a public garden. Every day we walked along the same path. Every day we sat on the same bench.

One day I noticed a young man in the garden. He was handsome, with black hair. His clothes were shabby. I guessed he was a student.

From then on, he was *always* in the garden when we were. We passed one another each day but never spoke.

The next year, the young man began to change. He dressed better. He sat on a bench closer to ours. He gazed shyly at Cosette.

When I saw Cosette return his gaze, I was upset. She was interested in him also!

I wanted my life with Cosette to go on forever. She was the only happiness I had ever known. I moved us to a new house. The walks in the garden stopped.

Cosette never said a word about the move. She missed our walks. And, I knew, she missed the young man. There was a kind of sadness in her now. Our life together was not as it once was.

But one day things changed. The young man, who had been out of our lives for months, came back.

I was standing outside the church one winter morning. A girl handed me a note from her father, "P. Fabantou."

Fabantou was an actor out of work. He asked me for money. He also asked me to come to his home. He wanted me to see how far he'd fallen.

I knew the address. It was the same building Cosette and I had lived in years ago! I said I would be there that afternoon.

I was nervous. Cosette and I had run from that old building with Javert on our heels. I never wanted to see that place again. But I had given my word.

The building was in even worse shape than before. It was hard to believe that people could live in it. But the streets of Paris are full of people without homes. Many of them would think it was a palace.

I tapped on Fabantou's door. It was opened by a small, bony man. He had the sharp stare of a weasel. Where had I seen his face before?

"Please come in, my dear sir!" he said, bowing low. "Please enter, with your charming young lady."

Cosette and I entered.

I found out later that Marius, the young

man from the garden, lived next door. At that moment, he was peering at us through a hole in the wall. He knew things about Fabantou that I was yet to learn.

No doubt Marius was shocked to see us. But here we were—the old gentleman and the girl he lost months ago. There she was before his eyes!

The room was like a cave—dark and cold. A window was broken and an icy breeze blew in. There was no fire in the fireplace.

Fabantou's wife was in bed with a cold. A girl sat on the floor by the bed. Her wrist was bleeding. It was wrapped in a piece of torn shirt.

These were truly *les misérables*—the outcasts, the underdogs. They were as I had been during my prison days. We were people that life destroyed.

"Here are blankets and woolen stockings," I said. I put a bundle on the table.

Fabantou asked me how he had signed his letter.

"It was signed 'Fabantou, the dramatic artist,' " I replied.

Only later did I learn that this wicked man used many different names. He wrote letters asking for money. He had a different story to go with each name.

"You see how we live, monsieur," said Fabantou. He swept an arm around the room as he spoke.

"The only rag of clothing I own is this torn shirt of my wife's. I can't go out to look for work because I have no coat. I owe a whole year's rent. Sixty francs! And it's due tomorrow!"

I pulled off my brown overcoat and laid it across the back of a broken chair. I gave him five francs.

"That's all the money I have on me," I said. "But I will be back at six with sixty francs for your rent."

Cosette and I left. We did not know that Marius ran after us. Our buggy had taken off before he reached the street.

Marius didn't have money for a buggy. He stood in the street and watched the girl he loved get away once more.

And Fabantou? I didn't know it then. Fabantou was setting a trap for me. I would walk freely into that trap, but barely escape with my life.

CHAPTER NINE

Trapped!

I was back at six o'clock with the money. Cosette was safe at home.

Fabantou greeted me wearing my overcoat and smiling meekly. I put eighty francs on the table.

"For your rent and other immediate needs, Monsieur Fabantou," I said. "We will talk about what else you need."

"May God reward you, most generous sir," said Fabantou. He snatched the money off the table.

I sat down. "How is the hurt child?" I asked.

"Not well," replied Fabantou. "She's in great pain. Her sister took her to the hospital."

"Madame Fabantou seems much better," I said, looking her way.

She was standing at the door with her arms crossed. She looked as if she would not let me leave if I wanted to.

"Oh, she's very sick," said Fabantou. "But you'd never know it. She's so brave. She's more than a woman—she's an ox."

Madame Fabantou was pleased by her husband's words.

"You always say the nicest things to me, Monsieur Jondrette." She smiled a shy smile.

"Jondrette?" I said. "I thought your name was Fabantou."

"It's both," said Fabantou, quickly. "Jondrette is my stage name."

I was beginning to see that things were not as they seemed. Then I noticed two men in the shadows.

"Who are those men?" I asked.

"Pay no attention to them," said Fabantou. "They're just neighbors."

"As I was about to say, my most noble patron," continued Fabantou. "I have a picture for sale."

There was a sound at the door. Two more men came into the room. They sat on the bed. The men's faces were covered in soot.

"Don't worry about them," said Fabantou. "They're furnacemen. They have dirty faces because they do dirty work. As I was saying, I want to show you a valuable picture."

Fabantou turned around a picture that

had been facing the wall. Light from the candle shone on it.

"What on earth is it?" I asked.

The men were watching me. I was uneasy.

"This is a masterpiece, my dear sir," replied Fabantou. "I cherish this picture as much as my own daughters. But sad to say, I am forced to sell it. What do you think it's worth?"

"It's an old inn sign," I said. "It's worth about three francs."

The paint was chipped and peeling, but I knew the sign. I could still make out THE SERGEANT OF WATERLOO in faint letters. Underneath the letters was a picture of a soldier carrying another soldier on his back.

It was hard to believe the man before me could be the innkeeper—the man called Thénardier.

"I will accept a thousand francs for this sign," he said.

I was caught in a trap. Escape wouldn't be easy.

"I won't accept one franc less. I hope you have your wallet on you."

The man grinned wickedly.

I rose from my chair and stood with my back to the wall. I looked around the room.

Thénardier stood near the window with two of the four men. His wife stood near the door with the other two. The trap was a tight one.

Suddenly Thénardier jumped at me. His eyes were blazing with anger. His fists were clenched.

"Don't you know me?" he screamed. "Don't you recognize me?"

"No," I replied calmly.

Just then the door swung open. Three more men entered, wearing black masks. One carried a heavy stick. The other had a butcher's axe.

"Is everything ready?" Thénardier asked them.

"Yes," said one of the men.

Thénardier came close, then thrust his face into mine.

"Don't you recognize me? My name isn't Fabantou or Jondrette. My name is Thénardier. Recognize me now?"

"No more than before," I replied. My eyes gave nothing away. I needed to buy time.

"Your goose is cooked, my noble patron!" Thénardier spat out the words. "You're spitted and roasted, my fine bird!"

He started to pace the room.

"You don't know me, eh?" he said. "It wasn't you who came to my inn in Montfermeil ten years ago and took Fantine's brat from me? So you don't know me! Well, I know you, all right.

"I knew you the minute you shoved your

75

noble face inside my door," he raged. "You'll not get away from me, my generous millionaire.

"It isn't smart to take a man's servant," he continued. "I'll teach you not to threaten me with a heavy stick. You were the strong one that day. Today it's my turn. I hold the cards now. And you're done for, my beauty!"

Thénardier stopped. He was out of breath.

"I don't know what you're talking about," I said. "I'm a poor man. I don't know you. You're confusing me with someone else."

"Have you anything to say before we go to work on you?" he replied.

I said nothing. What was the point?

The big man with the axe took his mask off. "If there's any chopping to be done, I'm your man!" he said.

Thénardier shouted at the man for

showing his face. In that instant, I ran for the window.

I was nearly out, but three men lunged at me. Six hands pulled me back inside.

I knocked down two of the men. But two more took their place. I was buried under a flood of fists.

"Don't hurt him!" shouted Thénardier. "I want to talk to this gentleman."

I was shoved into a chair.

"I find it strange," began Thénardier. "You haven't shouted for help once. Not even with the window open. I wonder. Are you as afraid of calling down the law as we are?"

I said nothing.

"We can help each other," continued Thénardier. "I'm not a bloodsucker. All I want is two hundred thousand francs. You don't have it with you. But you can write your daughter for it."

He turned to get paper and pen. I

lunged for the fireplace and grabbed the red-hot poker. I faced the room.

"You're a poor lot," I cried. "My own life is not worth much. You can do what you want with me. Look!"

I pulled up my left sleeve. I pressed the poker to my bare skin. There was a hiss of burning flesh.

"Poor fools," I said. "I don't fear you." I threw the poker through the open window.

"Do what you like with me," I said.

"Slit his throat!" cried one man.

Thénardier liked the idea. He picked up a knife from the table and started toward me.

CHAPTER TEN

Escape to Rue Plumet

Thénardier was almost upon me when suddenly his wife cried out, "Look at this!"

She handed him a balled-up piece of paper.

"How did this get here?" asked Thénardier.

"Through the open window," replied his wife.

"That's right," said one of the men. "I saw it go by."

Thénardier unfolded the note. He read it by candlelight.

"It's Éponine's handwriting, by God!" he exclaimed. "Our daughter writes, 'The police are here!' We better clear out! We'll leave the mouse in its trap."

But the mouse had dashed. I slipped through the window while everyone was busy with the note. I disappeared just as Javert opened the front door.

Thénardier and his gang were caught in their own trap!

Later I would learn how Marius saved my life. He had gone to the police that afternoon after overhearing Thénardier bragging to his wife about the trap he had set for me. And, amazingly, Éponine had printed the note for him that very morning, to prove that she could write!

When it looked as though Thénardier was going to kill me, Marius tossed the note through the hole.

I ran to my house on Rue Plumet. The house was protected by a stone wall. Cosette and the housekeeper lived there. I lived in a small cottage in the garden.

The next day I was sick with fever from the burn on my arm. Cosette nursed me with care. Everyday she brought me food. And everyday she read to me. I loved books about travel.

Cosette didn't ask me how I got the burn. She knew, from our years of secrets, when *not* to ask questions.

I thought life would return to the way it had been. Memories of the young man in the garden would grow dim with time. How happy I was at this thought. I felt reborn!

But things were not going to be like before. Everything was changing. Winter was giving birth to spring. And new ways were replacing the old.

"I want you to walk in our garden," I

said to Cosette one April morning. "You never go there."

"I will, Father," she replied. "Spring is such a wonderful time." She was happy again, and so was I.

I took my walks at night. That was the only time I felt safe enough to go into the streets. Just the same, I dressed as a workman. I felt even safer in my disguise.

One night I saw Thénardier in the street. He wasn't in prison after all. What was worse, the family lived in our part of the city—too close for comfort.

The next day I told Cosette we were moving. She grew sad. Her happiness of the last few weeks vanished. The garden had been good for her, but not for the reason I thought.

In the morning I found an address scratched on the stone wall. The letters were fresh.

They read: 16 RUE DE LA VERRERIE.

"This must be that young man's address," I thought. "He is seeing Cosette behind my back. And he knows we are moving, so he gives her his address."

That night I watched from my bedroom window. The lovers met in the garden. They greeted one another with such joy.

Now I knew why Cosette was so happy. She had been meeting her lover every night!

I discovered later that Thénardier's daughter Éponine knew the streets of Paris well. She had found our place and told Marius.

We couldn't move somewhere else in the city. We had to leave the country. We would move to England!

CHAPTER ELEVEN

At the Barricade

In that year of 1832 there was unrest in every quarter of Paris. People were speaking against the government. Students were planning revolution.

It was rumored that the popular leader, General Lamarque, was near death. He was the only man in the government who cared about the poor. When he died, Paris would explode.

Cosette and I would spend one last week at our apartment in Paris. Then we would board a ship and sail for England.

Cosette said she didn't want to leave France. Still, she helped me pack our few belongings.

Then General Lamarque died. On June 5, 1832, his funeral procession made its way through the streets of Paris. The spark was struck. The powder keg was set to blow.

On the evening of that same day, I wandered back to the house on Rue Plumet. I wanted to take a last walk in our garden. A street boy called to me. He had a note for Cosette. It was from her lover. I opened it and read it.

My grandfather will not agree to our marriage. We have no money, so we cannot be together. I have gone to the barricades to die for the revolution. When you read this, my soul will be very near and smiling at you. Remember me. I love you.

Marius Pontmercy

So my enemy would soon be dead. I didn't have to do a thing and he would be gone from my life! I put the letter in my pocket. I didn't want Cosette to know where Marius was.

But my heart was heavy. Now I knew how much they loved each other. Though they couldn't marry, their hearts would always be one.

From the date on the letter, I saw that Marius intended Cosette to read it the next morning. Perhaps there was still time.

I changed into my old National Guard uniform. I left the house fully armed, headed for Marius's barricade.

How could I know that I would meet two enemies there? One enemy wanted my daughter. The other wanted my freedom.

Yes, Javert was at the barricade. Our paths would cross once more.

The barricade was enormous—three stories high and seven hundred feet long. Built in front of an inn, it blocked the entrance to three streets.

Anything and everything went into building the barricade. Doors, screens, broken windows, bedroom furniture, stoves, chairs, pots and pans. Whatever was at hand.

Behind the barricade young men with guns waited for the king's soldiers to come down the street.

I got there at dawn, just as men with families were being sent home.

"There must be no unnecessary deaths," Marius was saying. "Those men with wives and children must leave at once."

"In another fifteen minutes it will be too late," said Enjolras, their leader. "The soldiers will be here."

I offered to stay and fight.

"Citizen, you are most welcome," said Enjolras. "But we are about to die."

I said nothing. I had faced death many times in my life.

Suddenly there was the sound of trumpets. The barricade was under attack!

"On guard!" cried Marius from the top of the barricade.

Another man on the barricade shouted, "When there are no more kings, there will be no more war!"

"Heads down and get back to the wall," shouted Enjolras. "All of you down on your knees."

The soldiers were firing at the barricade. The whole barricade was being hit with bullets. We were cloaked in a cloud of smoke.

I was certain Marius would be the first one shot. He was standing in the line of fire.

He didn't seem interested in protecting himself.

A soldier was posted on the roof nearby. He could see straight into our stronghold.

I took aim with my musket and fired. I struck the soldier's helmet. It clattered into the street, and the soldier ran off.

"Why did you fire at the helmet and not at the man?" asked Enjolras.

I said nothing. Killing wasn't as easy for me as it seemed to be for these young men.

A spy was tied up in the inn. Enjolras told me to go and check up on him. I entered the inn, and the spy turned to me. I knew the man.

"So here we are," he said.

It was Javert.

He asked for a drink. I held a glass to his lips. Then Enjolras came in and put a gun on the table.

"I haven't forgotten you," he said to Javert.

He turned to me. "The last man to leave this place will blow out this spy's brains."

"May I be that man?" I asked.

"All right," replied Enjolras. "You can have the spy."

I picked up the gun. Javert's eyes were upon me. I released him from the post, and we left the inn. His hands were tied behind his back so I helped him over the barricade. We walked down an alley.

"Take your revenge," said Javert when we stopped walking.

I took a knife out of my pocket.

"A knife to the heart!" exclaimed Javert. "You're right. That's your style."

I cut the ropes on Javert's wrists.

"You're free to go," I told him.

Javert was too stunned to speak. He stared at me openmouthed.

"I probably won't leave here alive," I

said. "But if I do, you can find me at number 7, rue de l'Homme-Armé. I live there under the name of Fauchelevent. Now go!"

After a few steps, Javert turned. "I would rather you killed me," he said.

"Clear out!" I cried.

When he was gone, I fired the gun into the air.

I went back to the barricade and reported, "The spy is dead."

But Marius wasn't at his post. He was lying on the pavement. A bullet was in his shoulder. He looked dead. But he was still breathing.

The king's soldiers would soon be on the barricade. I had to get Marius to safety!

CHAPTER TWELVE

In the Paris Sewer

The inn doors were bolted. The men were inside. They would finish the fight from there.

The soldiers were climbing the barricade. I lifted Marius on my back. There was so little time.

But how could we get away? The streets were blocked at every turn. Soldiers were posted on every street. Only a bird could fly from this trap.

I ran down the alley where earlier I

had taken Javert. Years ago I had run from him with Cosette. Now I was running again. That time I had found a way to escape by going up. I couldn't do that this time.

I looked on the ground. If only the earth would open up and swallow us. At any moment a soldier would think to check this alley. We would be caught and killed.

My eyes searched everywhere for a way out. Then I saw it—the iron grate at the edge of the road. It was half hidden by the paving stones.

I laid Marius on the ground. The grate was about two feet square. It was just big enough for me to crawl down and pull Marius through.

Soon Marius and I were underground. I replaced the grate. In seconds we had gone from midday to midnight. The clamor of battle was now a mumble above our heads. We were in the Paris sewer!

The channel was narrow. I could touch

both walls at the same time. The floor was wet under my feet. A foul stench hung in the air.

Slowly my eyes got used to the dark. We were under the heart of the city. There were two passages in front of me. One passage would lead to the country. The other would lead toward the Seine River, and death.

There was light to the left but I chose the right, the darkest part of the sewer. It went uphill and, I hoped, away from the city.

Marius's arms were around my neck. His feet dragged behind. I held both his arms with one hand, using my other hand to follow the wall.

Yesterday's rain lay in the center of the channel. I stayed close to the wall so I wasn't in water. I walked slowly, like a creature of the night.

I walked knowing there were pits in the sewer and we could be swallowed up at any moment. I walked knowing each step could be my last.

Questions raced through my mind. Would I find a way out in time? Would Marius bleed to death? Would I wander the sewer until I starved to death? I couldn't stop the questions.

Then the ground changed. We were walking downhill now. The stream washed around the heels of my shoes, not just the toes. Perhaps we were heading toward the Seine.

If this were true we would be washed into the river and drowned. The danger was great. But the danger behind us was greater. So I walked on.

Marius's cheek pressed against mine. His breathing was faint.

We finally came to the end of the channel. There was a grate above my head. I put Marius down and looked through his pockets. I found a slip of paper in his wallet.

Marius had written, "My name is Marius Pontmercy. My body is to be taken to the house of my grandfather, Monsieur Gillenormand." The address followed.

Now I knew where I would take Marius once I removed the grate. I could see the early evening sky through the iron bars.

But this grate was different from the other one. It was bolted. Only a key would open it. We had come to a dead end!

I was exhausted. I didn't have the strength to turn back. And Marius was near death.

Suddenly I felt a hand on my shoulder.

"We'll go halves," said a low voice.

I turned. It was Thénardier! He didn't recognize me. I stood in the shadows, and there was blood on my face.

"How are you going to get out?" Thénardier went on. "You have no way of unlocking the grate. But you've got to get away from here."

"That's true," I replied.

"So we'll go halves," he said.

"How do you mean?"

"You've killed a man," Thénardier pointed at Marius. "I don't know you. But I'm ready to help you. I have the key. Give me half of what you found on this dead man's body. Then I'll unlock the grate for you."

I couldn't believe it. Escape was in the hands of the wicked Thénardier! My good angel wore an evil disguise.

"I'll give you this rope," he continued. "You can tie a stone to it and drown the body in the river. So let's settle up. Here's the key. Where's the money?"

I had thirty francs in my waistcoat pocket. It was nothing. I spread the coins on a ledge in the wall.

"You didn't kill for much," said Thénardier.

Then he searched Marius's pockets. "It's

true," he said. "There is no more money. I guess you better go out. It's like a fare. You pay when you leave. You've paid. So you can leave."

He laughed. Then he bent to help me put Marius on my back. He put the key to the bolt. The bolt slid back and the grate opened without a sound.

I walked into the cool night air. Thénardier bolted the grate behind me.

At last I was outside! I laid Marius on the nearby riverbank. The darkness, stench, and horror were behind me.

I was washing my hands and face in the river when I sensed someone standing behind me.

I turned. The tall man behind me wore a long coat. He held a policeman's stick in one hand. In the half-light I saw who it was—Javert!

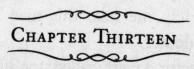

CHAPTER THIRTEEN

The Day That Follows Night

Javert didn't recognize me. He gripped his stick and stared.

"Who are you?" he asked calmly.

"Myself," I replied.

"And who is that?"

"Jean Valjean."

Javert put the stick between his teeth. He clapped a hand on my shoulder and leaned forward. Our faces nearly touched. He saw it was me.

He had chased Thénardier to the sewers. He had gone after a mouse and caught a lion!

"Inspector Javert," I said. "You have got me. I am your prisoner. Just grant me one thing. Help me take this man home. He needs a doctor."

Inspector Javert called for his carriage. His face was hard, like stone.

By the time we reached Marius's grandfather's house, it was late in the evening. Everyone was asleep. The doorkeeper let us in.

"There is still life in him," I said and laid the wounded young man on the couch.

I joined Javert in the buggy. But there was one more thing I needed to do. I asked him for one more favor.

"Let me go home for a minute. After that you can do what you like with me," I said.

Javert was silent for a moment. Then he

pulled down the window in front of him and said to the driver, "Drive to number 7, rue de l'Homme-Armé."

I wanted to tell Cosette that Marius was safe. I wanted to tell her where I kept my money. Then I would go with Javert. It was over for me.

"I'll wait for you here," said Javert when we had arrived.

I went upstairs to my room. Before calling Cosette, I looked out the window. To my astonishment, Javert was gone.

It was only later that I learned the truth. Javert threw himself into the Seine and drowned.

Maybe he couldn't bear to take me to prison. Maybe his duty to the law made it impossible for him to let me go. But I had spared his life, so he needed to spare mine.

You know the story from here, my dear Cosette. Now you know that the money I

gave you when you married Marius—
600,000 francs—was really mine to give.

I wasn't at peace living in your house
because of my secret. One day I took Marius aside. I told him I was an ex-convict.

Marius was stunned. "But what does it
mean?" he asked.

"It means I was a prisoner for nineteen
years," I said. "I escaped. I belong in prison
even now."

"But you didn't have to tell me," said
Marius. "You could have gone on living
with us under the name you were using—
Fauchelevent."

"I once stole a loaf of bread to stay
alive," I replied. "But now I cannot steal a
name in order to go on living.

"How would it be if someday we were all
out together and the police recognized me
and took me away?" I continued. "What
would Cosette think? No, it's better this
way."

But I made Marius promise not to tell you. I moved out of his house. He said I could visit every evening, and I did.

But Marius's welcome vanished. Soon I knew he didn't want me to come by. I missed an evening now and then. Finally, I stopped my visits.

I'm sorry I hurt you Cosette. I'm sorry I pulled away from you. I loved you like a father, yet I wasn't your father. I made you stop calling me "Father." I couldn't bear the lie anymore.

I saw the hurt in your eyes when I asked you to call me "Monsieur Jean."

Marius thinks I stole the money. Now you can tell him the truth. I was an outcast all my life. I have loved you, Cosette, for as long as I have known you. I did everything I could to make you happy.

Now I am finished. I am ready to die. I will lie down and wait for the end to come. It won't be long. Soon I will wake to a new day when this dark night is over.

The pen fell from Jean Valjean's fingers. He had given up on life. But he did not rest for long.

Suddenly someone knocked at the door. It was Cosette and Marius. They had come to see him.

Cosette rushed into the room. Marius stood in the doorway.

"Cosette," said Jean Valjean. He sat upright in his chair. His face was thin and pale. But his eyes were happy. Cosette ran into his arms.

"Father!" she cried.

"So have you forgiven me, my Cosette?" asked Jean Valjean.

Looking at Marius he said, "And you, too, have you forgiven me?"

Cosette's eyes filled with tears. Marius bowed his head.

"Thank you," said Jean Valjean. "I have

lived a hard life. Now I can die in peace."

Jean Valjean walked to his bed and lay down. He felt as though the world were slipping away from him.

Marius ran to his bedside.

"Now I know what you did for me," he said. "Why didn't you tell me? It is I who asks forgiveness of you."

Marius was on his knees. Cosette was kneeling too.

"You saved my life," said Marius. "Even more, you gave me Cosette! I can never repay you."

"You have no need to say all this," murmured Jean Valjean.

"You will not spend another day in this horrible place," said Marius. "You are Cosette's father and mine as well. You are part of us."

"Yes, Father," said Cosette. "You will come to live with us."

"Children, I am dying," whispered Jean

Valjean. "I will not live in this world much longer."

"You will not die," said Marius.

"People don't die just like that. You have suffered so much. But now your suffering is over. You must not only live. You must live with us."

"See, Father," said Cosette. "Marius says you aren't to die. We will be happy together."

Jean Valjean smiled.

"Come close to me, both of you," he said. "I love you dearly. How sweet it is to die like this."

The old man's eyes closed for the last time. Light from two silver candlesticks fell on his face.

Cosette and Marius kissed Jean Valjean good-bye. But he could not return their kiss.

Victor Hugo was born in France in 1802. He started writing when he was very young. He published his first book of poetry when he was only twenty and later wrote several successful plays and novels, including *The Hunchback of Notre Dame* and *Les Misérables*. Hugo's stories are best known for their characters—simple people who overcome great obstacles.

During the 1840s, Hugo became involved in French politics. When Emperor Napoleon III overthrew the government in 1851, Hugo fled France. Although he did not return for almost twenty years, his passion for writing never wavered. Victor Hugo, one of the best romantic writers of his time, died in France in 1885.

Monica Kulling was born in British Columbia, Canada. Ms. Kulling is the author of the Bullseye adaptation *Little Women*. Her credits also include two picture books and many poems published in *Cricket* magazine. She lives in Toronto, Canada, with her partner and their two dogs, Sophie and Alice.

ANOTHER SERIES YOU WILL ENJOY: